Saint Kett

The Bed Who Ran Away from Home

Dan Greenburg

illustrated by John Wallner

■ HarperCollins*Publishers*

To Kate,
Best wishes,
Dan G...
11/10/92

To Zack,

who never wants to go to bed

—D.G.

Sincere thanks to Lynda Cassanos

—J.C.W.

The Bed Who Ran Away from Home
Text copyright © 1991 by Dan Greenburg
Illustrations copyright © 1991 by John Wallner
Printed in the U.S.A. All rights reserved.
10 9 8 7 6 5 4 3 2 1
First Edition

Library of Congress Cataloging-in-Publication Data
Greenburg, Dan.
    The bed who ran away from home.

    Summary: A bunk bed feels rejected and runs away
from home when the twins who sleep on the top and
the bottom stay up past their bedtime.
    [1. Beds—Fiction. 2. Bedtime—Fiction. 3. Stories
in rhyme] I. Wallner, John C., ill. II. Title.
PZ8.3.G754Be 1991   [E]   87-35144
ISBN 0-06-022279-4
ISBN 0-06-022280-8 (lib. bdg.)

Once upon a time,
It is said,
There lived an exceptional
Double-bunk bed.

The bunk on the top
Of the bed was the same
As the one on the bottom,
And the bed had a name.

The name of the bed
That I speak of was Bosco,
Although I have heard
It preferred the name Rosco.

In the bed slept a boy
Whom his parents called Ned,
And his smart sister Nancy,
And a panda named Fred.

Now Ned had the top bunk
And Nancy the bottom,
And Fred slept with either,
Depending who got him.

And Bosco was happy at night
With his friends,
But something bad happens
Before my tale ends.

The bad thing that happened,
I'm sad to relate,
Began around bedtime
One night about eight.

Nancy and Ned
Were watching TV,
And their mother and father
Were drinking some tea,
When the telephone rang
And Mom went to answer,
And who should it be
But Aunt Zelda, the dancer!

Aunt Zelda, it seems,
Had returned from a tour
Of faraway places
Where she danced for the poor.

And while she told tales
Of Tangiers and Decatur,
The hour on the clock
Became later and later.

So Mom talked to Zelda,
While Dad read the news.
The time went unnoticed,
And Dad took a snooze.

Only Nancy and Ned
In the overstuffed chair
Knew how late it was getting,
And they didn't care.

They watched the TV,
And they hugged panda Fred,
And completely forgot
About Bosco, their bed.

But Bosco, I'm terribly
Sorry to say,
Did not forget *them*,
And it ruined his day,
And his night in addition,
And he made a low moan,
For his friends had gone off
And left him alone.

"Perhaps," Bosco thought,
As he watched the clock sadly,
"I was lumpy last night
And made them sleep badly,
And now they have found
A bed they like better,
And they've cast me aside
Like an old, worn-out sweater."

The hands on the clock
Showed eight forty-five,
And then it was nine,
But they didn't arrive.

And the clock struck nine thirty,
And what do you think?
A tear dropped from poor
Bosco's eye with a plink.

"If they don't come in here,
At the latest, by ten,
That means," Bosco thought,
"I won't see them again.

"I will slip out the window
And find some nice kid
Who will love me a lot
More than *these* children did."

So Bosco kept watch
By the clock on the wall,
While Mom was involved
With her telephone call.

Father continued
To snooze on the couch,
And Nancy and Ned
Continued to slouch
On the overstuffed chair
With their old panda Fred,
And no one at all
Even *thought* the word "bed."

So as the old clock
Struck the hour of ten,
Bosco went to the window
And had a strong yen
To just burst out crying,
But he was too proud,
So he slipped out the window
Without being loud.

"Well, Zelda," said Mother,
"I can't say that I'm—
Good Gracious! Good Heavens!
Just look at the time!"

"Good night, dear," said Zelda.
"We'll talk more at Grandma's."
"Good night," Mother said.
"Kids! Get your pajamas!"

"You mean that it's eight
And bedtime already?"
Said Nan and her naughty
Twin brother, Neddy.

"No, it's two hours *later*,"
Said Mother. "Now hurry
And run off to bed,
Or Mother will worry."

"Okay, Mom," they said,
And stood up with a grin
And went to their bedroom,
But when they walked in
The smiles on their faces
Dissolved in a trice.
They looked around once.
They looked around twice.

"Help, Mother! Help, Father!"
They yelled, "It's so weird—
Our sweet little Bosco
Has just disappeared!"

Their mother and father
Rushed in through the door,
Took a quick look about,
And their jaws hit the floor.

"I do not believe
What my eyes tell me now.
Your bed," said their mother,
"Went away, but, well, *how?*"

"I have no idea of *how*,"
Said young Ned,
"But I think I know *why*
We lost our nice bed."

"Then tell us," said Father,
"My fine little scholars—
For a new one will cost
About three hundred dollars."

"I think that poor Bosco
Left for one reason only.
Because," Nancy said,
"He must have been lonely."

"I think what she's saying,"
Said Ned, "is quite true.
But what in the world
Can the two of us do?"

"We will get a new bed
In a week, more or less.
You could sleep on the couch
In the meantime, I guess,"
Said Father, which made
Both children bawl:
"If we can't have our Bosco,
We want no bed at all!"

"Whatever you like,"
Father said,
"That's the score.
Perhaps you'd prefer
To sleep on the floor?"

And oddly enough,
Though their mom nearly wept,
That is exactly
Where those children slept.

They wrapped themselves up
In quilts worn and patchy,
And two heavy blankets
That were woolly and scratchy.

The floor was quite hard,
But they slept nonetheless.
It was well past eleven
By then, I would guess.

They dreamed of their Bosco
Showing defiance
To hideous monsters
And bed-eating giants.

Just after midnight
They awoke with a fright.
They sensed there was something
Outside in the night.

"Oh, Nancy!" cried Ned.
"Call Mommy, I'm scared!"
But Nan knew that girls
Were young women who dared.

She crept to the window
And climbed onto the sill.
"Be careful!" called Neddy.
Said Nancy, "I will!"

And before you could say,
"Oh, jinkies! Go hide!"
Brave Nancy had flung
The big window wide.

"Who's out there?" she called
In a voice loud and clear,
And the next thing she knew
A black shape had drawn near.

It was big, black, and scary.
It sure wasn't human.
And its voice, when it spoke,
Was creepy and boomin'.

"Are there kids in this house?"
The black shape inquired.
"What *of* it?" said Ned,
In a voice he admired.

"What *of* it?" said Nancy,
Echoing Neddy.
The shape seemed impressed
That their voices were steady.

"The reason I ask,"
The big, black shape cried,
"I'm a bed and I'm lonesome
Without kids inside."

"It's Bosco!" yelled Ned,
Though the black shape said "Whom?"
And both children helped him
Climb into their room.

"Are you glad that
I'm back?" said the unhappy bed.
"Oh, Bosco, we *missed* you,"
Said Nancy and Ned.

"In that case I might
Even stay for a while,"
Said Bosco, and smiled
A sad little smile.

The children and Fred
Went to bed with much laughter,
And all of them lived
Happily ever after.